Postman Pat's
Washing Day

Story by John Cunliffe
Pictures by Joan Hickson

From the original Television designs by Ivor Wood

Hippo

Scholastic Children's Books,
Commonwealth House, 1-19 New Oxford Street,
London, WC1A 1NU, UK
a division of Scholastic Publications Ltd
London ~ New York ~ Toronto ~ Sydney ~ Auckland

First published in the UK, 1988
This edition published by Scholastic Ltd, 1997

Text copyright © Ivor Wood and John Cunliffe, 1988
Illustrations copyright © André Deutsch Children's Books, Scholastic Ltd
and Woodland Animations Ltd, 1988

ISBN: 0 590 19556 5

Made and printed in Belgium by Proost

2 4 6 8 10 9 7 5 3 1

It was a sunny Wednesday morning in Greendale. Breezy, too. Pat was on his way with the letters.

"It's a good day for Granny Dryden's washing day," said Pat to Jess. Jess wasn't bothered about the weather. He had a wash every day. A quick lick and a paw behind the ears kept him clean.

When Pat arrived at Granny Dryden's cottage, there was no washing on the line.

"That's funny," said Pat. "No washing out. She always has it out good and early. I hope she's not poorly."

Pat knocked at the door, and called,
"Morning! Letters!"
And there was Granny Dryden, sitting
by the fire, knitting.

"No washing?" said Pat. "You've not forgotten it's Wednesday, have you? And it's a grand day for washing. Sunny and windy. It would dry in no time."

"Oh, no, Pat, I've certainly not forgotten," said Granny Dryden. "But that new machine of mine has gone and broken down, so I'm just getting on with a bit of knitting. And there's a basketful of washing waiting to be done."

"I know what we can do," said Pat.
"Mrs. Pottage does her washing on a
Thursday. If I put your washing
basket in my van, I can ask her to pop
your washing in with hers, when I call
with the post tomorrow. I'm sure she'd
not mind. She has a big washing
machine and plenty of hot water."
"Oh, Pat, that is kind," said Granny
Dryden.

Pat was on his way. When he called at
Thompson Ground there was no
washing out there, either.
"You're missing a good drying day,"
said Pat to Dorothy Thompson.

"The washing will have to wait," said Dorothy. "If I don't get this baking done, there'll be nothing for tea." Dorothy's kitchen was full of good smells. Pat had a hot buttered scone with his cup of tea.

There was no washing out at the
vicarage, either. The Reverend Timms
was in his study, but he came out for
his post.

"I thought you'd have some washing on the line, on a grand day like this," said Pat.

"Quite right, Pat," said the Reverend. "The good Lord sent such a day for drying washing. But I have to write a sermon for Sunday, and if I don't do it today I'll never do it."

And the Reverend went back to his writing.

"Dear me," said Pat. "Is nobody doing their washing?"

Ted Glen was busy mending his
Landrover, so he did no washing.

Miss Hubbard was busy with her bees,

so she did no washing.

George Lancaster was putting up a new hen-house, so he did no washing.

"I hope Mrs. Pottage does her washing tomorrow," said Pat.

The next day was Thursday. When Pat called on Mrs. Pottage, the kitchen was full of washing smells, and the machine was swooshing and rumbling away with a full load. So he told Mrs. Pottage about Granny Dryden's washing.

"Bring it in," said Mrs. Pottage, "there's plenty of hot water."

"No trouble," she said, when she saw
Granny Dryden's washing. "Just put it
down there. Would you like a cup of
tea, Pat? The kettle's just boiled."
"Thanks," said Pat. "That would be
lovely."

It was hot in Mrs. Pottage's kitchen.
Pat took off his hat and jacket, and
laid them on a chair. Then he sat down
for his tea.

He didn't see Mrs. Pottage tipping Granny Dryden's washing out of the basket, and on to a handy chair.

Mrs. Pottage didn't see Pat's hat and jacket on the chair.

The washing machine finished its load.
Mrs. Pottage took the clean clothes
out. She put Granny Dryden's
washing in.

"It'll be done in no time," she said.
"I'll pop in for it when I've delivered
my letters," said Pat. "She'll want to
hang it out while it's still sunny.
Thanks. I'll be on my way."

But, when Pat went to get his hat and jacket, they weren't there! They looked all over the kitchen for them.

Then Mrs. Pottage began to laugh.

"There they are!" she said.

"What?" said Pat.

"In the washing machine."

Pat's hat and jacket were whizzing round and round with Granny Dryden's washing.

"How did they get there?" said Pat.
"You have to watch me on wash-day,"
said Mrs. Pottage. "You can't put
anything down. It all goes in."
"They needed a wash," said Pat.

"It's a bit chilly," said Mrs. Pottage.

"I'll lend you something of Herbert's."

Pat went on his way, in Mr. Pottage's second-best tweed jacket, and deer-stalker hat. He didn't look at all like a postman.

On Friday, Pat took Granny Dryden her clean washing. She was very pleased to see it.

"You look as though you've been in the wash as well," she said. "You're looking very smart."

"It wasn't all bad luck," said Pat, "your machine breaking down." And he told her what had happened.

"And I've asked Ted to pop in and see if he can mend your machine," he said.

"Oh, it's all right now," said Granny Dryden. "I'd only forgotten to plug it in. No wonder it wouldn't go. But don't tell Ted not to come. I haven't seen him for ages. We can have a good chat, and he can tell me all about his sister's wedding."

And that's what happened. Ted was
bringing the wedding photographs,
anyway, as well as the egg-whisk he'd
mended months ago and forgotten all
about.